A catalogue record for this book is available from the British Library

Published by Ladybird Books Ltd
27 Wrights Lane London W8 5TZ
A Penguin Company

Stories in this book were previously published by Ladybird Books Ltd in the *Favourite Tales* series.

MY LADYBIRD BOOK OF

10 BEDTIME TALES

Ladybird

Contents

Cinderella
based on the story by
Charles Perrault
retold by Nicola Baxter
illustrated by Jon Davis

Sleeping Beauty
based on the story by
Charles Perrault
retold by Nicola Baxter
illustrated by Gavin Rowe

Little Red Riding Hood

based on the story by
Jacob and Wilhelm Grimm
retold by Nicola Baxter
illustrated by Peter Stevenson

Rapunzel

based on the story by
Jacob and Wilhelm Grimm
retold by Nicola Baxter
illustrated by Martin Aitchison

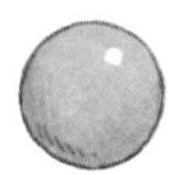

The Princess and the Pea

based on the story by
Hans Christian Andersen
retold by Nicola Baxter
illustrated by Robert Ayton

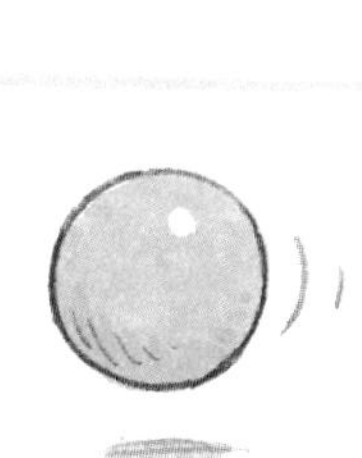

Hansel and Gretel

based on the story by
Jacob and Wilhelm Grimm
retold by Audrey Daly
illustrated by Peter Stevenson

Snow White and the Seven Dwarfs

based on the story by
Jacob and Wilhelm Grimm
retold by Raymond Sibley
illustrated by Martin Aitchison

The Ugly Duckling

based on the story by
Hans Christian Andersen
retold by Lynne Bradbury
illustrated by Petula Stone

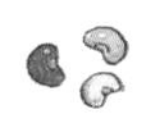

Jack and the Beanstalk

based on a traditional folk tale
retold by Audrey Daly
illustrated by Martin Salisbury

Thumbelina

based on the story by
Hans Christian Andersen
retold by Audrey Daly
illustrated by Petula Stone

cover and borders illustrated by
Peter Stevenson

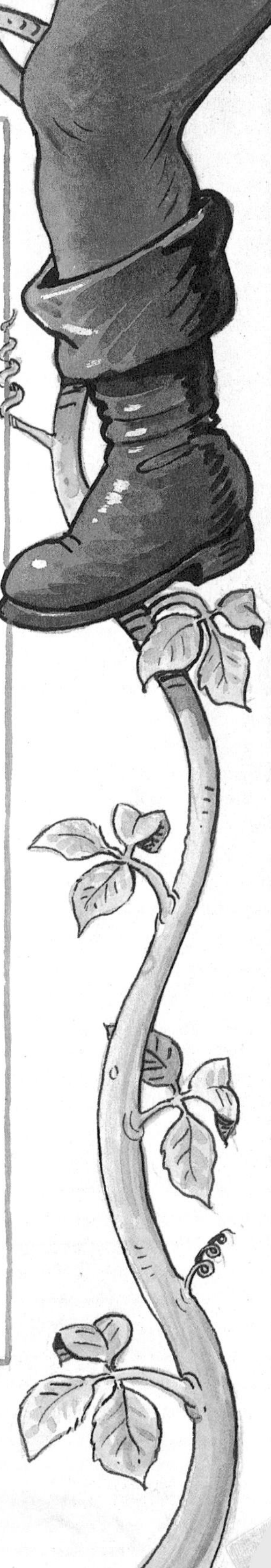

Cinderella

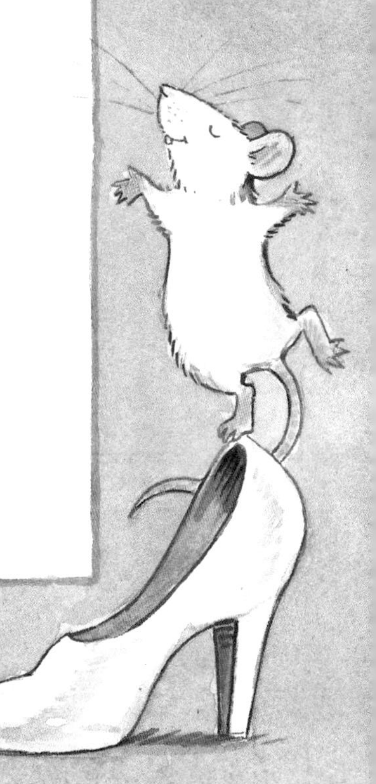

Once upon a time there was a young girl called Cinderella.

She lived with her father and two stepsisters. While her stepsisters spent their time buying pretty new clothes and going to parties, Cinderella wore old, ragged clothes and had to do all the hard work in the house.

The two sisters were selfish, unkind girls, which showed in their faces. Even wearing their fine clothes, they never looked as sweet and pretty as Cinderella.

One day a royal messenger came to announce that there was to be a grand ball at the King's palace.

The ball was in honour of the Prince, the King's only son.

Cinderella's sisters were both excited. The Prince was very handsome, and he had not yet found a bride.

When the evening of the ball arrived, Cinderella had to help her sisters get ready.

"Fetch my gloves!" cried one sister.

"Where are my jewels?" shrieked the other.

They didn't think for a minute that Cinderella might like to go to the ball!

When her sisters had driven off in their fine carriage, Cinderella sat all by herself and cried bitterly.

“Why are you crying, my dear?” said a voice. Cinderella looked up and was amazed to see her fairy godmother smiling down at her.

“I wish *I* could go to the ball and meet the Prince,” Cinderella said, wiping away her tears.

“Then you shall!” laughed her fairy godmother. “But you must do exactly as I say.”

“Oh, I *will*,” promised Cinderella.

“Then go into the garden and fetch the biggest pumpkin you can find,” said the fairy.

So Cinderella found an enormous pumpkin and brought it to her fairy godmother. With a wave of her magic wand, the fairy changed the pumpkin into a wonderful golden coach.

"Now bring me six white mice from the kitchen," the godmother said. Cinderella did as she was told.

Waving her wand again, the fairy godmother changed the mice into six gleaming white horses to pull the coach! Cinderella rubbed her eyes in amazement.

Then Cinderella looked down at her old ragged clothes. “Oh dear!” she sighed. “How can I go to the ball in this old dress?”

For the third time, her godmother waved her magic wand. In a trice, Cinderella was wearing a lovely white ballgown trimmed with blue silk ribbons. There were jewels in her hair, and on her feet were dainty glass dancing slippers.

“Now off you go!” said her fairy godmother, smiling. “Just remember one thing – the magic only lasts until midnight!”

So Cinderella went off to the ball in her sparkling golden coach.

In the royal palace, everyone was enchanted by the beautiful girl in the white and blue dress. “Who *is* she?” they whispered.

The Prince thought Cinderella was the loveliest girl he had ever seen.

“May I have the honour of this dance?” he asked, bowing low.

All the other girls were jealous of the mysterious stranger.

Cinderella danced with the Prince all evening. She forgot her fairy godmother's warning until... *dong... dong... dong...* the clock began to strike midnight... *dong... dong... dong...*

Cinderella ran from the ballroom without a word... *dong... dong... dong...*

In her hurry, she lost one of her glass slippers... *dong... dong... dong*. The Prince ran out just as the lovely girl slipped out of sight.

"I don't even know her name," he sighed.

When Cinderella's sisters arrived home from the ball, they could talk of nothing but the beautiful girl who had danced with the Prince all evening.

"You can't imagine how annoying it was!" they cried. "After the wretched girl left in such a hurry, he wouldn't dance at all!"

Cinderella hardly heard their complaining. Her head and her heart were whirling with memories of the handsome Prince who had held her in his arms.

Meanwhile, the Prince was determined to find the mysterious beauty who had stolen his heart. The glass slipper was the only clue he had.

"The girl whose foot will fit this slipper shall be my wife," he said.

So the Prince set out to search the kingdom for his bride. A royal messenger carried the slipper on a silk cushion.

Every girl in the land wanted to try on the slipper. But although many tried, the slipper was always too small and too dainty.

At last the Prince came to Cinderella's house.

Each ugly sister in turn tried to squeeze her foot into the elegant slipper, but it was no use. Their feet were far too big and clumsy.

"Do you have any other daughters?" the Prince asked Cinderella's father.

"One more," he replied.

"Oh no," cried the sisters. "She is much too busy in the kitchen!" But the Prince insisted that *all* the sisters must try the slipper.

Cinderella hung her head in shame. She did not want the Prince to see her in her old clothes. But she sat down and tried on the dainty slipper. Of course, it fitted her perfectly!

The Prince looked at Cinderella's sweet face and recognised the girl he had danced with. "It *is* you," he whispered. "Please be my bride, and we shall never be parted again."

How happy Cinderella was! Her fairy godmother appeared and, waving her magic wand, dressed Cinderella in a gown fit for a princess.

Then the Prince led Cinderella home to the royal palace.

Cinderella and her Prince were married at the most magnificent wedding that anyone could remember. Kings and queens from many lands came to meet the new Princess and wish her well.

Even Cinderella's sisters had to agree that she was the loveliest bride they had ever seen.

And Cinderella and her Prince lived happily ever after.

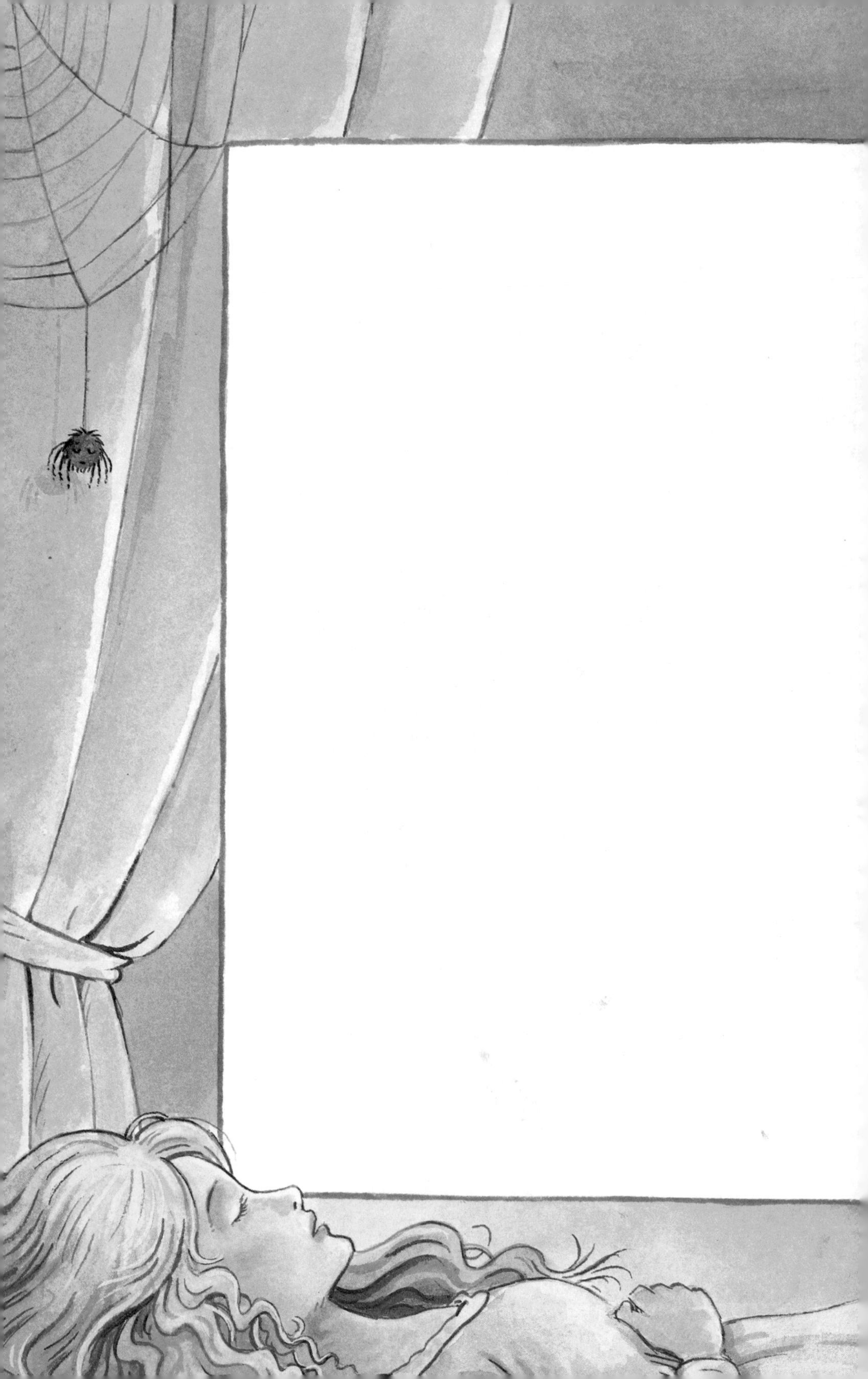

Sleeping Beauty

Once upon a time there was a king and a queen who had long hoped for a child of their own. When, at last, a baby princess was born, they thought that a good fairy must have been looking after them.

“I shall invite all the fairies in the kingdom to come to our baby’s christening!” cried the King joyfully.

When the time for the christening came, the King was as good as his word.

Among the guests were the twelve good fairies who lived in that land. After the grand feast, each of them gave a magic gift to the baby girl.

“You shall have a lovely face,” said the first.

“You shall be gentle and loving,” said another.

One by one, they promised the little Princess all the good things in the world.

When eleven of the fairies had given their gifts, a furious voice was heard at the doorway.

“I suppose you thought I was too old to do magic now! Well, I’ll show you!” it shrieked. And a very old fairy, whom everyone had forgotten, walked slowly towards the cradle.

“When the Princess is fifteen years old, she shall prick her finger on a spindle and fall down dead,” she cursed, and rushed from the palace.

The King was horrified. “Oh, how can I have forgotten her?” he cried. “And what shall we do now?”

“I may be able to help,” said a gentle voice.

It was the twelfth fairy. “I can’t undo the evil spell,” she said, “but I can soften it a little. The Princess will prick her finger on a spindle, but she will not die. She will just fall asleep for a hundred years.”

The King and Queen were very grateful to the twelfth fairy, but still they did not want anything to happen to their precious daughter. They made sure that all the spindles in the kingdom were destroyed.

Year by year, the Princess grew more lovely. Surely no one could want to harm such a kind and gentle girl?

On the morning of her fifteenth birthday, as the Princess wandered through the palace, she climbed to a high tower where she had never been before. There she saw a wooden door.

Pushing it open gently, she peeped inside. There sat an old, old woman at a spinning wheel.

"Good morning," said the Princess. "What are you doing?"

"I am spinning, my child," said the old woman. "Look!" and she handed the Princess the sharp spindle. At that moment, the Princess pricked her delicate finger!

At once, the Princess fell into a deep, deep sleep. The wicked fairy's words had come true.

At the same moment, everyone in the palace fell asleep as well.

In the great hall, the King and Queen fell asleep on their golden thrones.

The lords and ladies, the palace guards, and all the servants fell into a deep slumber. The whole palace was silent and still.

As the years passed, a hedge of thorns and brambles grew up around the palace walls. It grew so tall and so thick that at last only the flags above the highest towers could be seen.

The story of the beautiful sleeping Princess spread through the kingdom and far beyond.

She became known as the Sleeping Beauty.

Many princes came to the palace, hoping to rescue the Princess, but none could force his way through the thick, sharp thorns.

Almost a hundred years had passed since the Princess had pricked her finger, when a handsome young Prince from a faraway kingdom happened to pass by.

On the road he met an old man, who remembered a story that his grandfather had told him. And so it was that the Prince heard the legend of the Sleeping Beauty.

“I shall not rest until I have seen her and woken her,” he vowed.

When the Prince saw the great hedge of thorns, he nearly despaired. But when he raised his sword, the thorns suddenly turned into lovely roses, and the hedge opened to let him through.

Inside the palace gates, all was still. The dogs lay asleep in the courtyard. The guards slept at their posts. Even the pigeons sat asleep on the rooftops. Not a sound could be heard.

The Prince searched the entire castle. He found the sleeping King and Queen and their sleeping servants. But it was not until he reached the very last room in the highest tower that he found Sleeping Beauty herself.

He gazed at her lovely face in wonder. "I would give my whole kingdom if you would wake and be my bride," he whispered.

Then he bent over and gently kissed
the sleeping girl.

At the touch of the Prince's lips, Sleeping Beauty awoke. As she smiled at him, she felt as if she had loved him all her life.

Throughout the palace there were sounds of laughter. Everyone woke and rubbed their eyes. They could hardly believe that the evil spell had been lifted at last.

As for Sleeping Beauty and her Prince, they were married soon after. And the King made sure that *everyone* was invited to the wedding!

Little Red Riding Hood

Once upon a time there was a little girl who loved to visit her grandmother. The old woman was always busy making something for her favourite granddaughter.

One day she made something very special indeed. It was a beautiful, bright red cape with a hood. The little girl loved it so much that she wore it all the time!

Soon everyone started calling her "Little Red Riding Hood".

One morning the little girl's mother said, "Little Red Riding Hood, your grandmother is not very well. I am packing up some things to help her feel better and I'd like you to take them to her.

"But *do* be careful as you walk through the forest. And *don't* stop for anything on the way!"

"I'll be *very* careful," promised Little Red Riding Hood, "and I won't stop for a second."

So off she went with her little basket. She waved to her mother until she was out of sight.

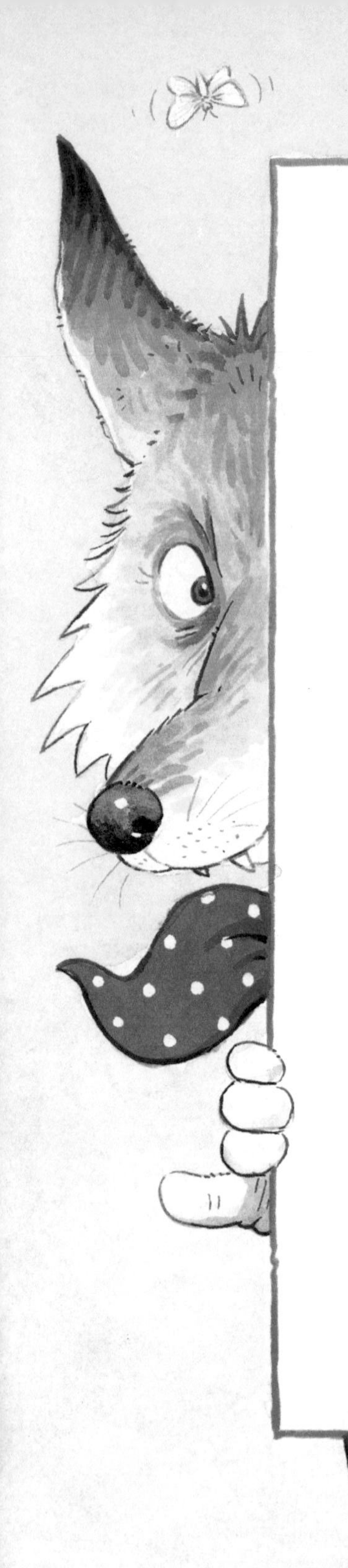

Just at the edge of the forest, a very crafty fellow was waiting.

It was a wolf! When Little Red Riding Hood passed by, he greeted her with a slow smile.

"Good morning, my dear," he said. "And what a fine morning it is!"

Little Red Riding Hood had never met a wolf before, so she wasn't scared. "Good morning," she said politely, "but I'm afraid I can't stop and talk."

"No matter, my dear," said the wolf. "I shall walk along with you. Where are you off to, this fine morning?"

"I'm going to see my grandmother," replied Little Red Riding Hood.

"Then I think I can be of service," said the wolf. "I'll show you where there are some lovely flowers, my dear. You can take her a bouquet."

Little Red Riding Hood knew that she shouldn't stop, but she did like the idea of taking her grandmother a special present. So she followed the wolf.

"Here we are," he said. "Now I must fly. I am late for my lunch."

When Little Red Riding Hood reached her grandmother's house, she was a little bit surprised to see that the door was open.

"Is that you, my dear?" croaked a faint voice. "Do come in!"

But when Little Red Riding Hood crept up to her grandmother's bed, a very strange sight met her eyes.

"Oh, Grandmother!" she cried. "What big ears you have!"

"All the better to hear you with, my dear," came the reply.

Little Red Riding Hood went a little closer.

"Oh, Grandmother! What big eyes you have!" she gasped.

"All the better to see you with, my dear!"

Little Red Riding Hood took one more step.

"Oh, Grandmother! What big teeth you have!"

"All the better to eat you with!" cried the wolf, and he gobbled her up!

When Little Red Riding Hood did not come home that afternoon, her parents were very worried. At last her father went to Grandmother's cottage to find her.

How horrified he was when he found a fierce animal in Grandmother's bed! With one blow of his axe, he killed the wicked wolf.

Then Little Red Riding Hood's father carefully cut open the wolf. Out jumped the little girl! She felt very strange indeed.

"Where is Grandmother?" she asked.

"I'm in here!" cried a muffled voice from inside the wolf. Little Red Riding Hood and her father soon pulled the old lady out and tucked her up in bed.

"I feel a lot better now!" said Little Red Riding Hood's grandmother, as she tasted the good things the little girl had brought.

Little Red Riding Hood's mother was so glad her little girl was safe that she hadn't the heart to scold her.

"I know you won't stop to pick flowers next time, Little Red Riding Hood," she said, "because *I* will give you some to take to Grandmother!"

Rapunzel

Once upon a time, in a faraway land, there lived a man and his wife. They had a pretty little house and all that they needed, but one thing made them unhappy.

"If only we had a child of our own to love and look after," they sighed.

Next to their house stood an old mansion with a beautiful garden. People said that a wicked witch lived there. One day, the wife glimpsed some lettuces growing in the next-door garden.

Although she went on with her work, the lettuces stayed in her mind. Finally, she said to her husband, "I feel I shall die if I don't taste one of those crisp, green lettuces. Won't you please climb over the wall and get one for me?"

Her husband was afraid to go into the garden, so at first he refused. But as the days passed, the wife's yearning for the lettuces grew, until at last she became quite ill.

One night, the man could bear it no longer, and he climbed over the wall. As his feet touched the ground, he nearly fainted with fright. There before him stood the witch.

"How dare you come creeping into my garden?" she snarled.

"I must have some lettuces for my wife," the man pleaded. "She is ill, and she will die without them."

"Take the lettuces, then," said the witch. "But in return, you must give your firstborn child to me."

The man was so terrified that he agreed. Grabbing a handful of lettuces, he fled back to his wife.

Some time later, a beautiful baby girl was born to the man and his wife. That same day, the witch appeared at their door. Reminding the man of his promise, she took the baby away.

The witch named the child Rapunzel, and she looked after her well. Every year the girl grew more lovely.

So that no one should ever see how beautiful she was, the witch shut Rapunzel up in a high tower in the forest. The tower had no door and no staircase – just one window right at the top.

Only the witch ever visited poor Rapunzel. She would call out,

"Rapunzel, Rapunzel,
Let down your hair."

Rapunzel's hair shone like gold in the sun, and it was so long that it reached from the top of the tower right down to the ground.

Huffing and puffing, the wicked witch would slowly climb the tower, holding on to Rapunzel's lovely hair. Then she would climb in through the window.

Years passed, and Rapunzel never set eyes on another living person. Then, one day, a young prince riding through the forest heard Rapunzel's sweet singing.

“I have never heard such a lovely voice,” he said to himself. “I shall not rest until I find out who it belongs to.”

So the Prince hid nearby and saw the witch climb the tower.

That evening, after the witch had gone, the Prince called out,

"Rapunzel, Rapunzel,
Let down your hair."

Rapunzel was astonished to see a young man climb through the window. And the Prince was dazzled by the lovely girl. As they spoke to each other, they realised they were in love.

"I will come back tomorrow night to rescue you," the Prince promised.

When the witch returned the next day, she saw at once that Rapunzel's heart was full of love for a stranger.

"You have betrayed me, you wicked girl!" she shrieked furiously. With her sharp scissors, she went *snipper snap!* and cut off Rapunzel's hair. Then she took the girl to a distant desert and left her there, alone and weeping.

The witch returned to the tower to wait for the Prince. At last she heard him call,

"Rapunzel, Rapunzel,
Let down your hair,"

and she lowered the golden plait for him to climb.

When the Prince found himself face to face with the angry witch, he leapt in despair from the tower. He fell into a thicket of briars, which scratched his eyes and blinded him.

For years the Prince wandered through many lands, until one day, in a lonely desert, he heard the lovely voice that he had never forgotten.

“Rapunzel!” he cried, throwing his arms around her. Rapunzel’s tears of joy fell on the Prince’s eyes and healed them. Once more he saw her beautiful face.

The Prince took Rapunzel's hand and led her to his kingdom, where they were married with great rejoicing.

And there, safe at last from the wicked witch, Rapunzel and her Prince lived happily ever after.

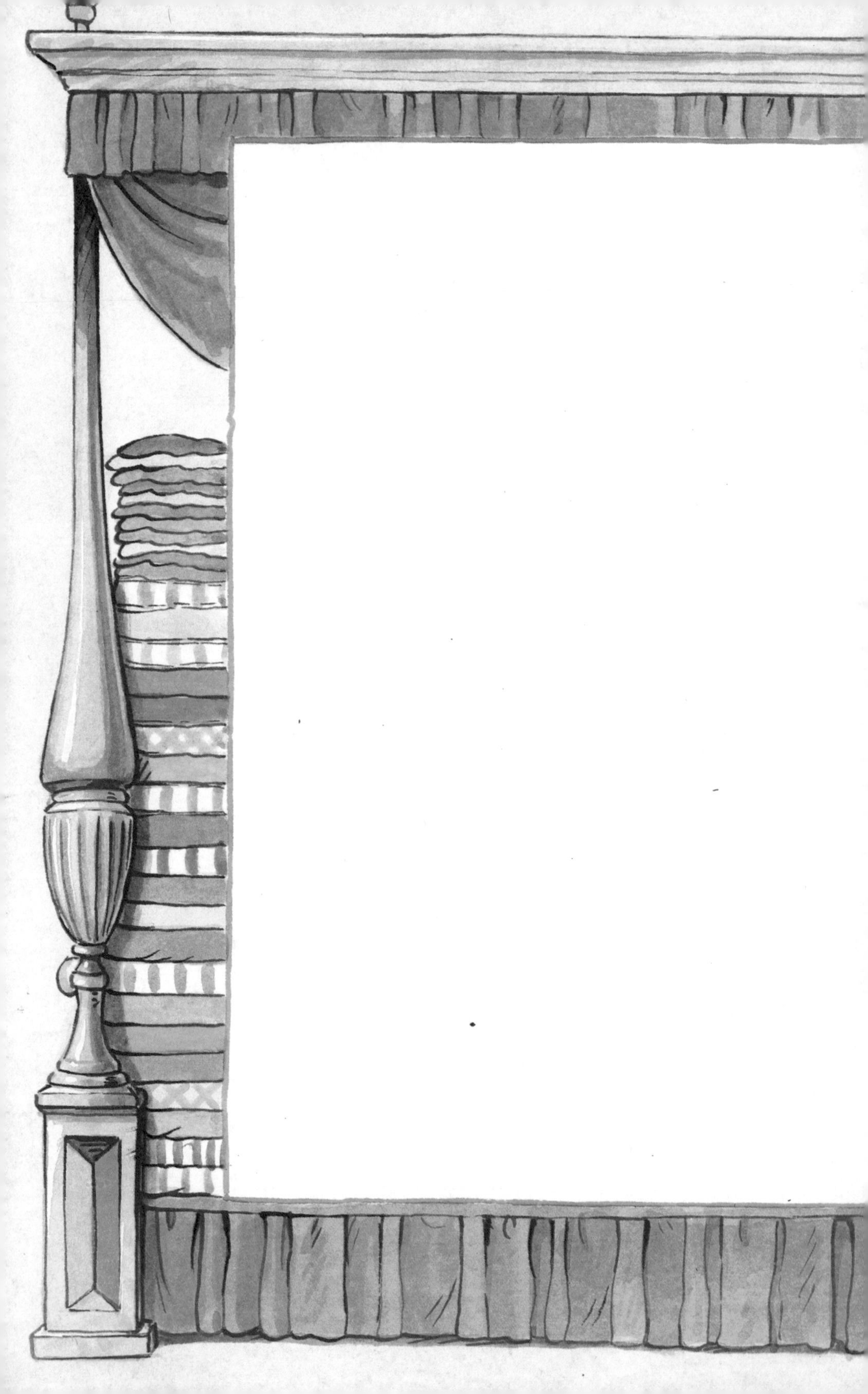

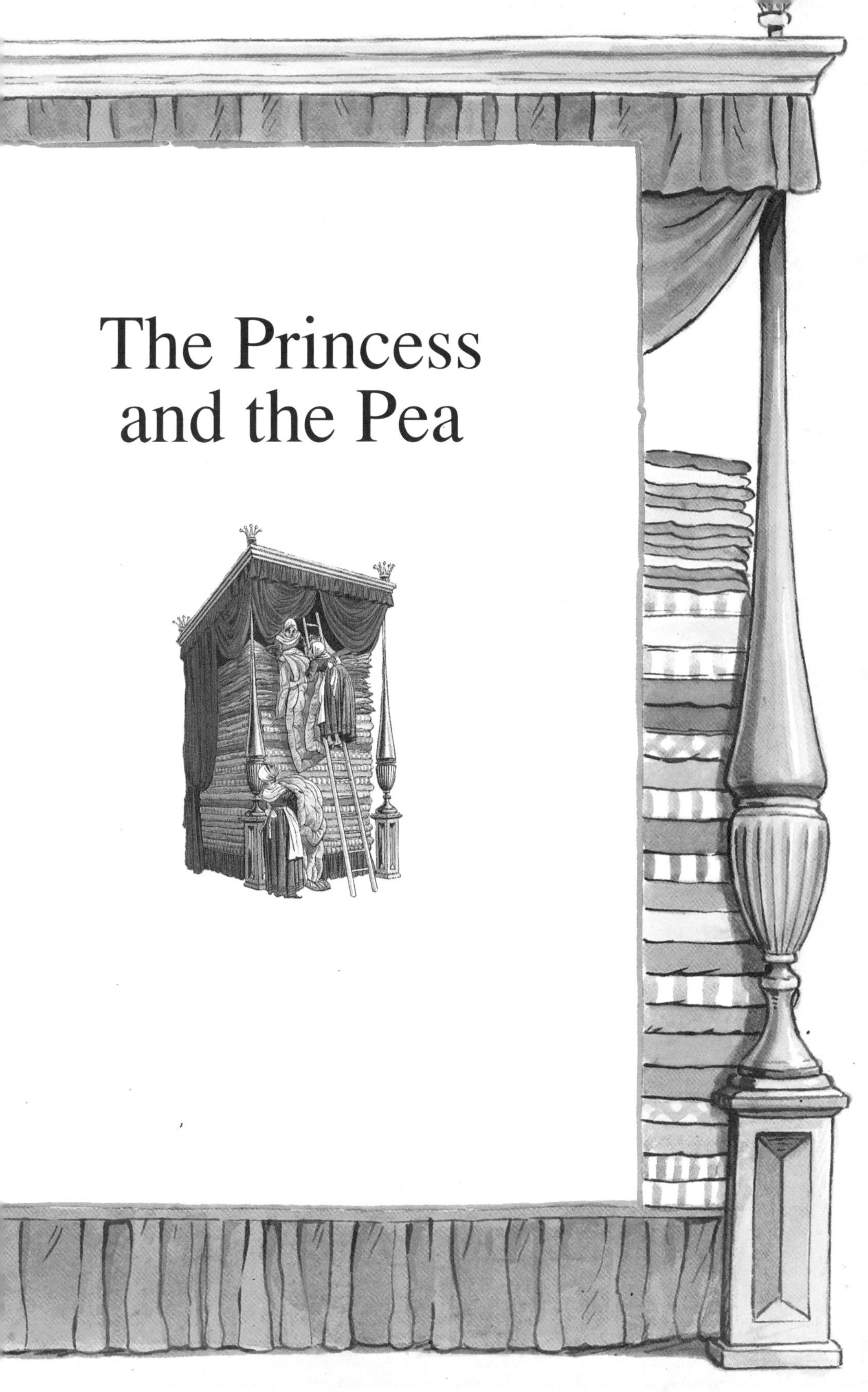

The Princess and the Pea

Once upon a time, in a kingdom far away, there lived a handsome young prince. The time had come for him to find a princess to marry.

"She must be a *real* princess," the Prince told the King and Queen. "That is the most important thing of all."

So the Prince rode off to search for a real princess.

He travelled far and wide for many years. Whenever he saw a castle, he stopped to find out if a real princess lived there.

On his travels, the Prince met many clever and beautiful ladies, but he was never quite sure if they were *real* princesses. For a real princess is a very special person, and there are very few of them to be found.

At last, sad and lonely, the Prince returned home.

One night a terrible storm raged around the castle where the Prince lived with the King and Queen. Rain beat against the old stone walls, and thunder roared overhead.

As lightning flashed across the sky, a small figure struggled through the rain and knocked on the castle door.

Inside, all the servants were hiding, frightened of the storm. The King himself went to see who was knocking on such a wild night.

The King was astonished to see a beautiful young girl standing outside! She was shivering with cold, and dripping from head to foot.

"My dear, come in at once!" cried the King. He led the lovely stranger to the warm room where the Queen and the Prince were waiting.

As soon as he saw her, the Prince fell in love with the beautiful girl.

He was filled with happiness when she curtsied and said, "Your Majesties, I am a *real* Princess."

"Well, well," thought the Queen, "we'll soon find out whether she's a *real* princess." While the lovely visitor put on dry clothes, the Queen herself went to see that a comfortable bed was made ready.

Right at the bottom of the bed, on the very first mattress, the Queen put a tiny green pea. Then she said, "Bring more mattresses! Hurry!"

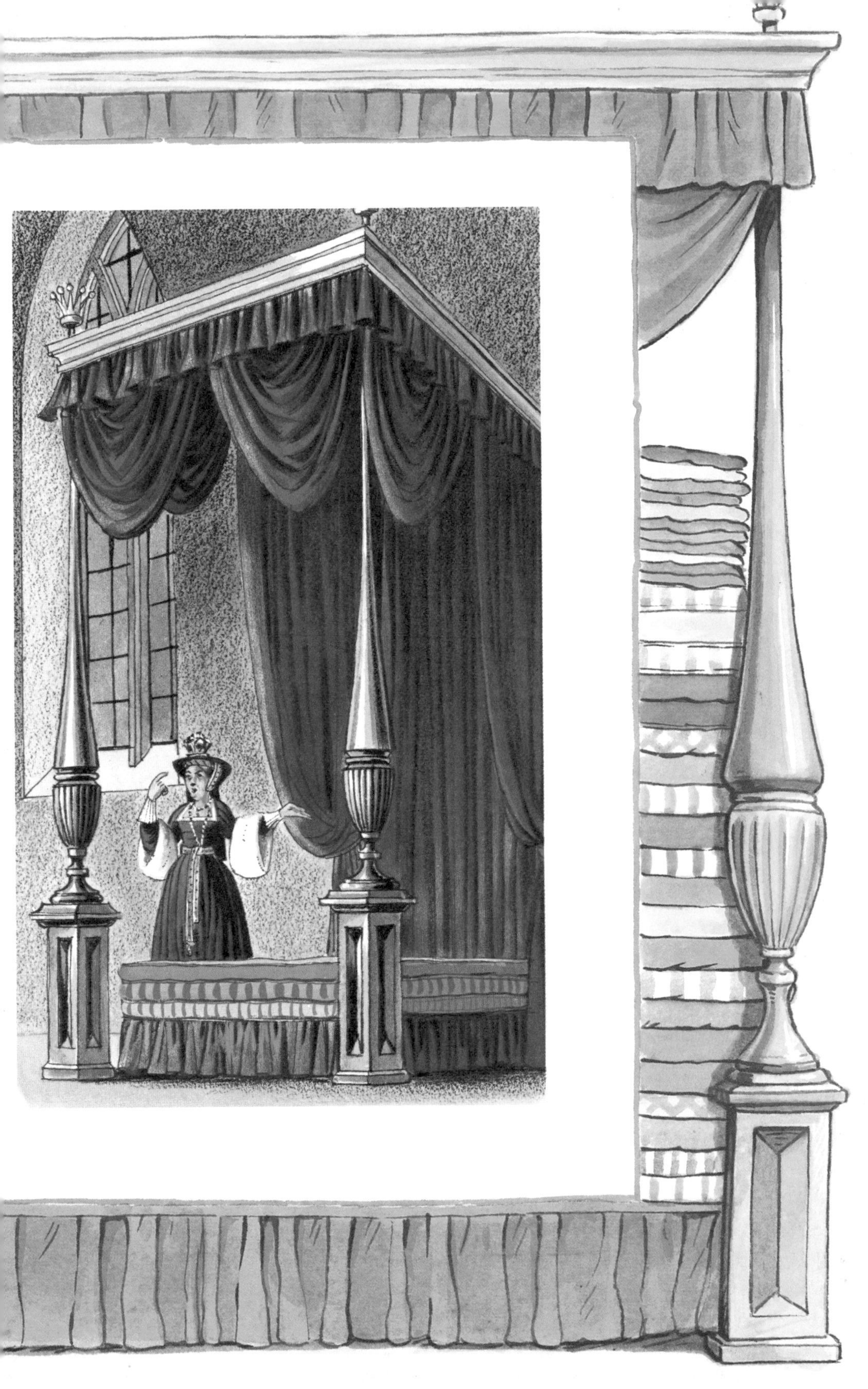

At last the bed was ready. There were so many mattresses that a ladder was needed to reach the top!

"I hope you will have a comfortable night, my dear," said the Queen, leading her visitor to bed.

In the morning, the Queen hurried to find out if her plan had worked.

The young girl was already awake and sitting up in bed.

“Did you sleep well, my dear?” asked the Queen.

"I'm afraid I didn't sleep at all," the girl replied. "There was something hard in the bed, and it has made me black and blue all over."

The Queen smiled. "Only a *real* princess would have such delicate skin that she could feel a pea through so many mattresses," she said.

When the Queen told the Prince the news, he was overjoyed. "At last I have found you!" he told the Princess. "Please say you will be my bride."

The Princess shone with happiness. "I will," she whispered.

So the Prince and the Princess were married, amid great rejoicing.

As for the pea, it was put in a museum. People came from far and near to look at it.

"You see," they said to each other, "our princess is a *real* princess. She is a very special person indeed!"

Hansel and Gretel

Once upon a time, a boy called Hansel and his sister Gretel lived with their father and stepmother in a cottage near a forest.

They were so poor that they sometimes did not have enough to eat. One day the children heard their stepmother say to their father, “Tomorrow we must take the children deep into the forest and leave them there. Otherwise *we* shall starve.”

Gretel was frightened, but Hansel had a plan. That night, when everyone was asleep, he crept outside and filled his pockets with shiny white pebbles.

The next morning, when the family went into the forest, Hansel walked more slowly than the others. When no one was looking, he dropped his pebbles along the path.

As soon as they were deep in the forest, their stepmother left the children by themselves, telling them to wait until someone came to fetch them. They waited until it grew dark, but no one came.

At last the moon rose. Hansel showed Gretel the pebbles he had dropped. They shone white in the moonlight and showed the children the way home.

When the tired, hungry children arrived back at the cottage, their father was very glad to see them.

But their stepmother was angry. Next day she told the woodcutter that they would have to take the children into the forest again.

"And this time we must see that they *can't* find their way home!"

That night, when everyone was asleep, Hansel got up to collect some pebbles again. But his stepmother had locked the door and hidden the key. Hansel could not get out.

In the morning, before they all set off, their stepmother gave the two children a small piece of bread each for their lunch.

They hadn't gone very far before Hansel began to walk more slowly than the others.

“Why are you so slow?” his stepmother shouted, looking back at him. “Hurry up!”

“I’m only saying goodbye to my friends the birds,” said Hansel. But he was really stopping to drop breadcrumbs along the path.

When they had gone deep into the forest, the woodcutter lit a small fire for his children. Sadly, he told them to wait beside it until someone came to fetch them.

The children waited until it grew dark, but no one came.

When the moon rose, Hansel and Gretel looked for the trail of breadcrumbs to lead them home.

But there wasn't a single crumb to be seen. The birds had eaten them all!

The children tried to find their way out of the forest, but they didn't know which path to take. They were completely lost.

Hansel and Gretel were tired and frightened and very, very hungry. They had no idea where to go or what to do next.

Suddenly Gretel cried, "Hansel, look!" Just ahead of them was a strange little house made of cakes and gingerbread, with a roof of sugary icing.

Laughing with pleasure, the children broke off bits of the house and began to eat.

Suddenly the door of the little house creaked open. An old woman looked out.

"Hello, children," she said, smiling. "Come inside, and I will give you food and somewhere warm to sleep."

The children went into the house, and she gave them some delicious pancakes and milk. In the back room there were two little beds.

Hansel and Gretel were happy to be safe at last with such a kind woman. They didn't know that she was really a wicked witch who liked to eat little children!

Next day the witch put Gretel to work scrubbing the floors. Then she took poor Hansel and locked him in a cage. “I’m going to fatten you up and eat you!” she cackled. “I’m looking forward to that!”

Every morning the witch, who had very poor eyesight, told Hansel to hold out his finger so that she could feel how fat he had grown.

But each time clever Hansel held out a chicken bone instead.

"Not nearly fat enough yet," the witch would mutter.

Days went by, and Hansel kept holding out a chicken bone instead of his finger.

At last the witch grew impatient. “I’m not waiting any longer! He *must* be fat enough by now,” she said one morning. “Today I’m going to cook Hansel and eat him. Gretel, light the oven.”

With tears in her eyes, Gretel did as she was told.

“Now, climb in and see if the oven is hot,” the witch ordered.

But Gretel was sure that the witch was trying to trick her. “I can’t climb into the oven,” she said. “I’m much too big.”

“Of course you can,” said the witch angrily. “Look, I’ll show you.” And she bent down and stuck her head in the oven.

Gretel didn’t waste a second. She gave the witch a hard push and slammed the door. The witch screamed with rage, but she couldn’t get out.

When Gretel was sure the witch was dead, she unlocked Hansel's cage and let her brother out.

"We're free!" she cried. "We can go home now!"

But first Hansel and Gretel searched the witch's house from top to bottom. In the attic, they were amazed to find chests full of pearls and rubies and diamonds.

"We must take some of these home to Father," said Hansel.

As the children set off, Hansel saw a white dove flying high above. “It’s one of my friends showing us the way!” he said.

Soon the children saw their own cottage through the trees. Their father was overjoyed to see them.

“Your stepmother has gone, and she is never coming back,” he said, hugging the children.

When he saw the jewels, the woodcutter couldn’t believe his eyes. “We’re rich!” he cried. “And we shall never be parted again.”

And they never were.

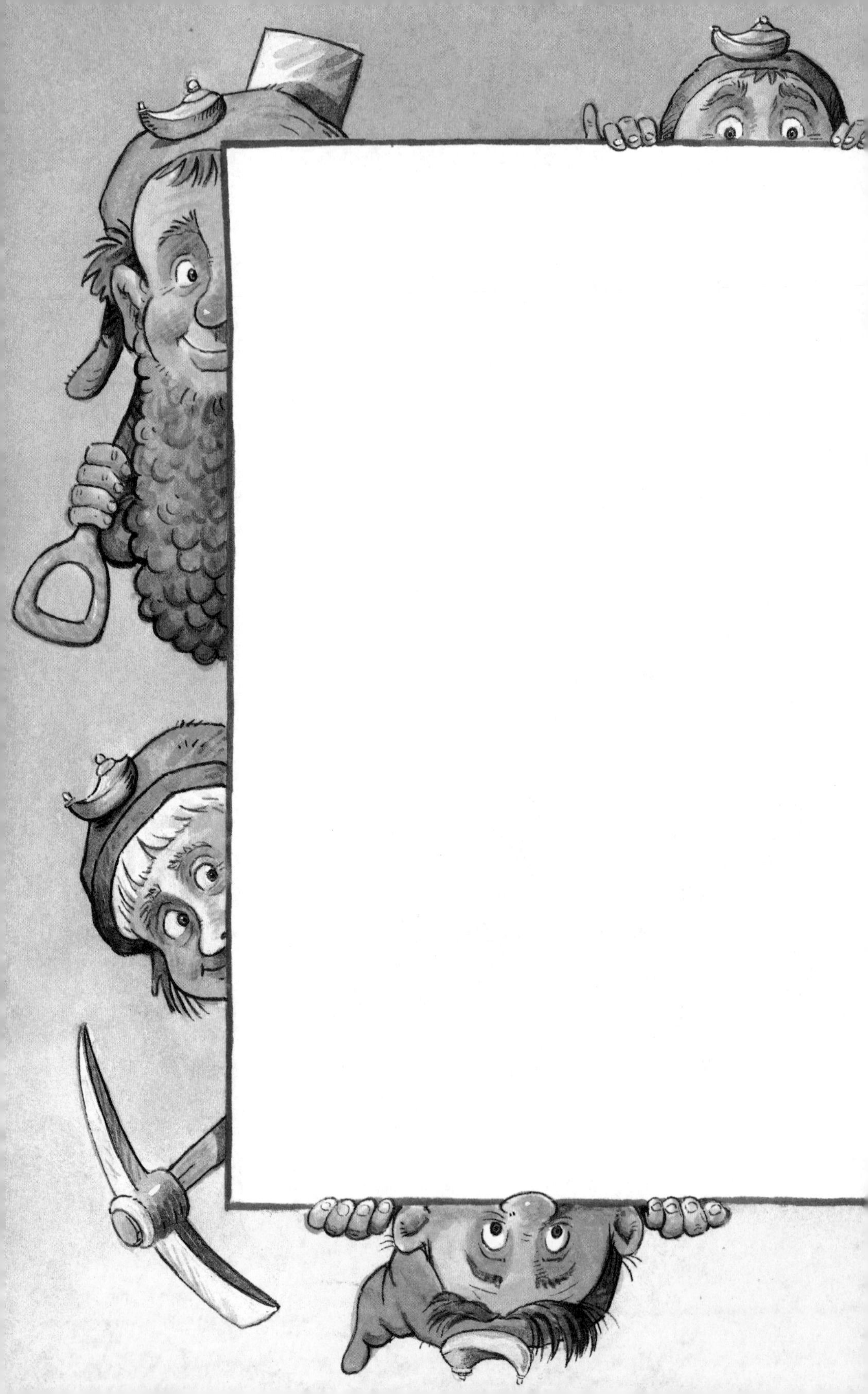

Snow White
and the Seven Dwarfs

One snowy day, a queen sat sewing at her window. As she glanced through the black ebony window frame, she pricked her finger and three small drops of blood fell upon her sewing.

The Queen sighed. “I wish I had a baby girl with cheeks as red as blood, skin as white as snow and hair as black as ebony,” she said.

Soon afterwards, her wish came true. She had a lovely baby daughter with red cheeks, white skin and black hair. She named the baby Snow White.

But before long the Queen died, and Snow White's father married again.

The new Queen was beautiful, but she was vain and selfish too. Her dearest possession was a magic mirror.

Every day the Queen would stand in front of her mirror and ask,

"Mirror, mirror, on the wall,
Who is the fairest of us all?"

And the mirror would reply,

"Thou, O Queen, art the fairest of all!"

But Snow White was growing up and becoming more lovely every day.

One day, when the Queen asked,

“Mirror, mirror, on the wall,
Who is the fairest of us all?”

the mirror gave a new reply.

“O Queen, Snow White is fairest of all!”

The Queen grew pale with rage.

From that day on, the Queen hated Snow White with all her heart. Every day the girl grew more and more beautiful. In her fury, the Queen sent for a huntsman.

"Take Snow White into the forest," she ordered. "Kill her and bring her heart back to me."

So the huntsman took Snow White into the forest, but he could not kill the lovely girl. “Run,” he said gruffly, “and never return!”

Snow White was lost and frightened. “Oh where shall I go?” she wept. At last she glimpsed a little cottage in a clearing.

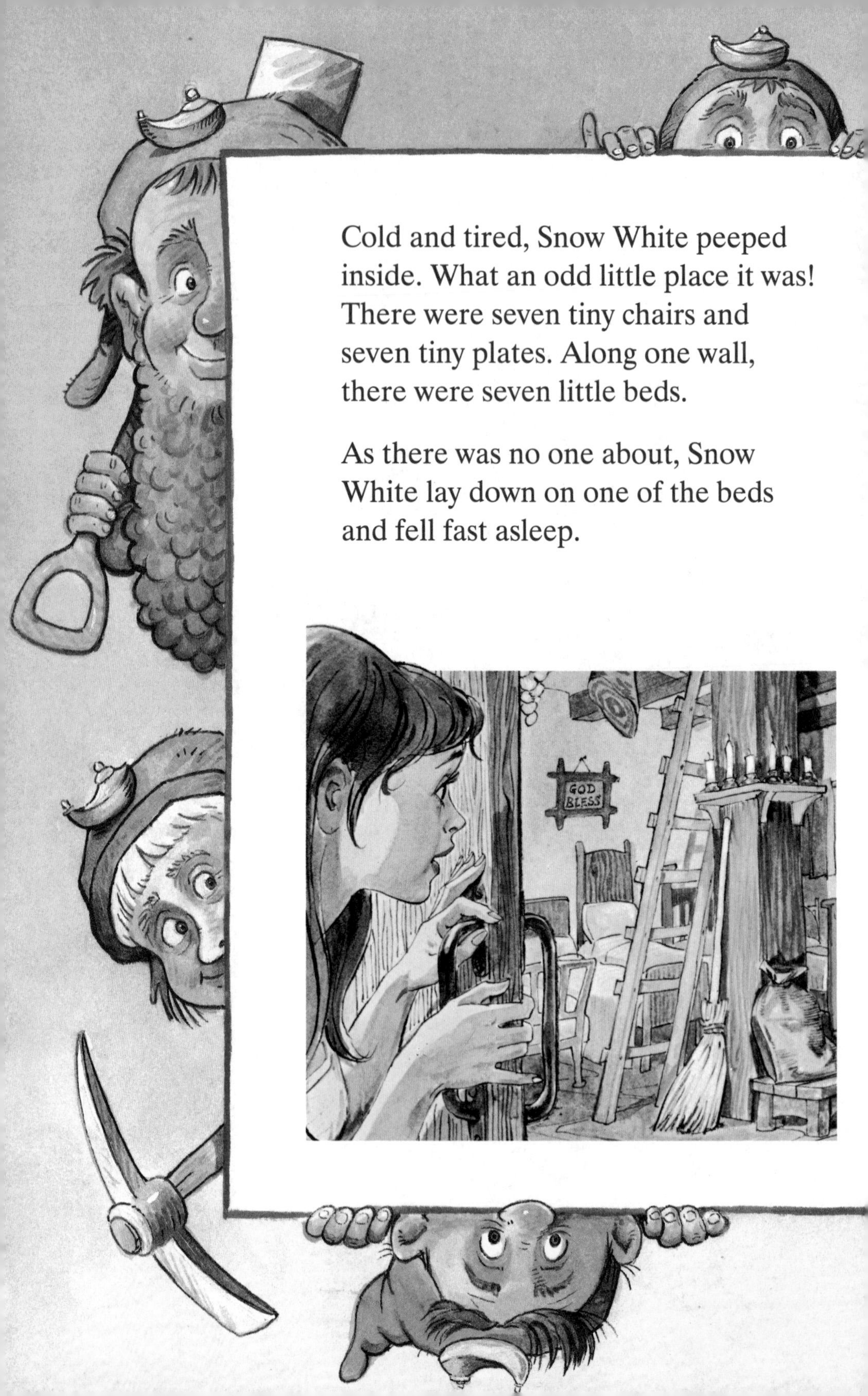

Cold and tired, Snow White peeped inside. What an odd little place it was! There were seven tiny chairs and seven tiny plates. Along one wall, there were seven little beds.

As there was no one about, Snow White lay down on one of the beds and fell fast asleep.

Unknown to the sleeping girl, the cottage belonged to seven dwarfs, who worked in the mines all day. At nightfall, they came home from their work and lit seven candles.

"Goodness me, there's someone here!" cried one of the dwarfs in surprise, when he saw Snow White.

The noise woke Snow White, and the seven little dwarfs crowded round her. “How beautiful she is!” they cried.

“Why have you come here, my dear, and how can we help you?” asked one of the dwarfs in a gentle voice.

Snow White explained about the wicked Queen. As she told her story, she grew so sad that she began to cry.

"Hush, my dear," said the kind little men. "You can live here with us, safe from that evil woman." Snow White gratefully accepted their offer.

In the palace, the Queen once again stood before her magic mirror. She did not know that the huntsman had disobeyed her and brought her an animal's heart instead of Snow White's.

Rubbing her hands with glee, the Queen smiled and said,

"Mirror, mirror, on the wall,
Who is the fairest of us all?"

And the mirror replied,

"O Queen, Snow White is fairest of all.
For in the forest,
where seven dwarfs dwell,
Snow White is still
alive and well."

Screaming with rage, the Queen planned her revenge.

Next morning, after the dwarfs left for work, Snow White sang happily to herself as she tidied the little house.

Before long an old pedlar woman knocked at the door. It was the Queen in disguise. “Come and look at these pretty things, dear child,” she cackled.

Snow White was enchanted.

She let the old woman tie a pink velvet ribbon around her neck to see how it would look. Suddenly, the old woman pulled the ribbon tight! Snow White fell to the ground.

The dwarfs found Snow White lying close to death. They untied the ribbon so she could breathe, and by the next morning she was well again.

"That pedlar was the wicked Queen!" said the dwarfs. Before they left for work, they made Snow White promise never to open the door to anyone.

Meanwhile, once again, the magic mirror had told the wicked Queen that Snow White was not dead.

The angry Queen disguised herself as
a kind old lady selling combs. Again,
Snow White nearly died, for the
combs were poisoned.

This time the dwarfs were very cross. “Do not let *anyone* into the house,” they said firmly.

When the mirror told the Queen that she had failed again, she was furious. She was determined that Snow White should die.

Next day the Queen took a basket of poisoned apples and tapped on the cottage window.

“I don’t need to come in,” she said cunningly, “but do try this lovely apple, dear child. It’s delicious!”

Snow White could see no harm in a shiny red apple, so she took a big bite.

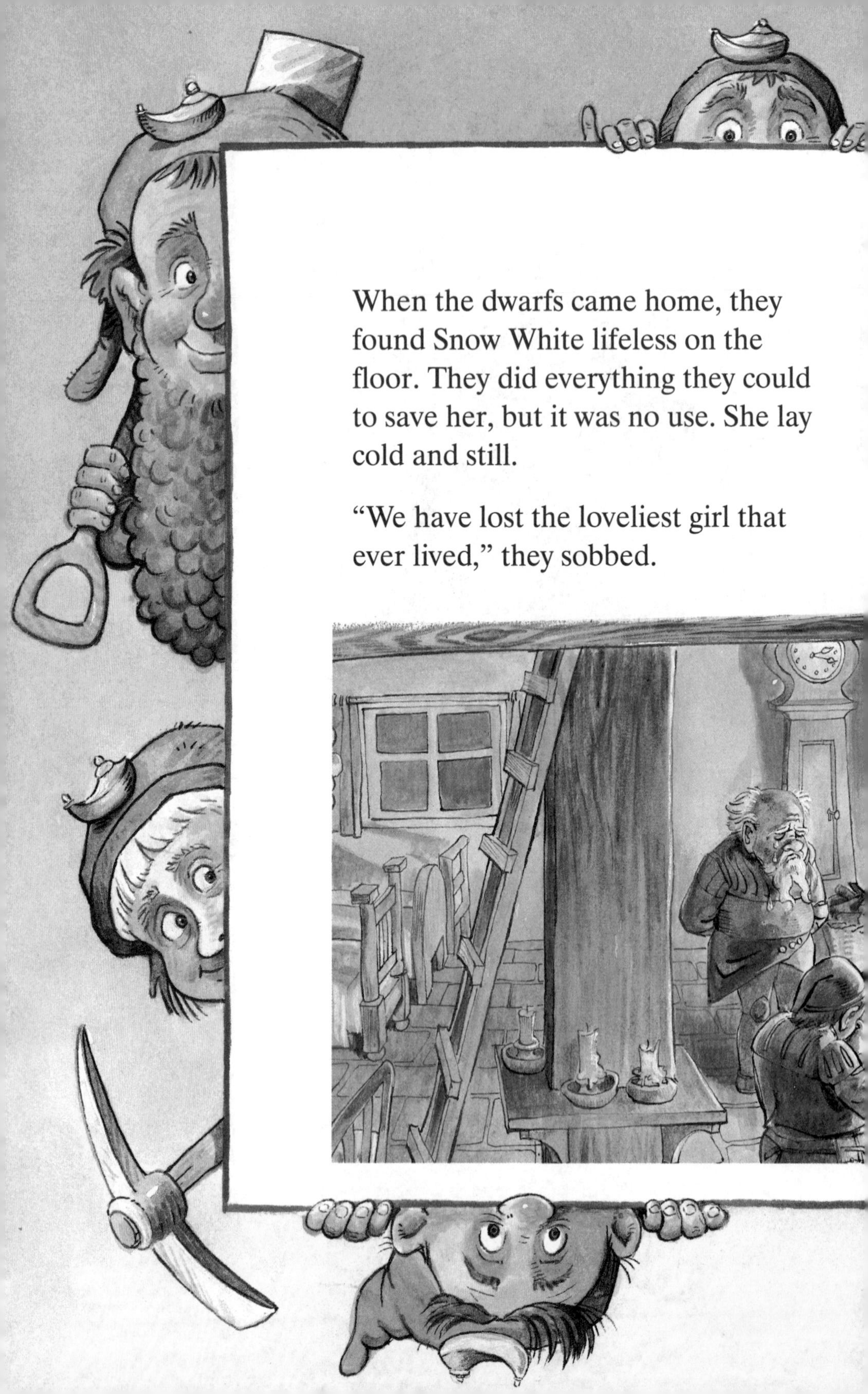

When the dwarfs came home, they found Snow White lifeless on the floor. They did everything they could to save her, but it was no use. She lay cold and still.

“We have lost the loveliest girl that ever lived,” they sobbed.

Far away in the palace, the Queen stood proudly before her mirror.

"Mirror, mirror, on the wall,
Who is the fairest of us all?"

And the mirror answered at last,

"Thou, O Queen, art the fairest of all."

The dwarfs could not bear to part with Snow White. Her cheeks were still as red as blood, her skin was as white as snow and her hair was as black as ebony.

So the little men made a glass coffin and laid Snow White's body tenderly in it. She looked for all the world as though she were only sleeping.

Day and night, the dwarfs kept watch beside the coffin. One evening, a young prince rode by.

As soon as he saw Snow White, he fell in love with her. "I beg you to let me take her home with me," he said, "so that she can lie in a palace as she deserves."

At long last, the dwarfs agreed.

As the Prince's servants were carrying the coffin down the mountain, they stumbled. Suddenly a piece of apple, which had been caught in Snow White's throat, fell out!

Snow White opened her eyes and saw the handsome Prince. "I love you," he whispered. "Please say that you will marry me." Snow White smiled happily.

The dwarfs, overjoyed that their beloved Snow White was alive, waved goodbye as she rode off with the Prince.

Soon Snow White and her prince were married. They lived happily ever after – and the wicked Queen and her mirror were never heard of again!

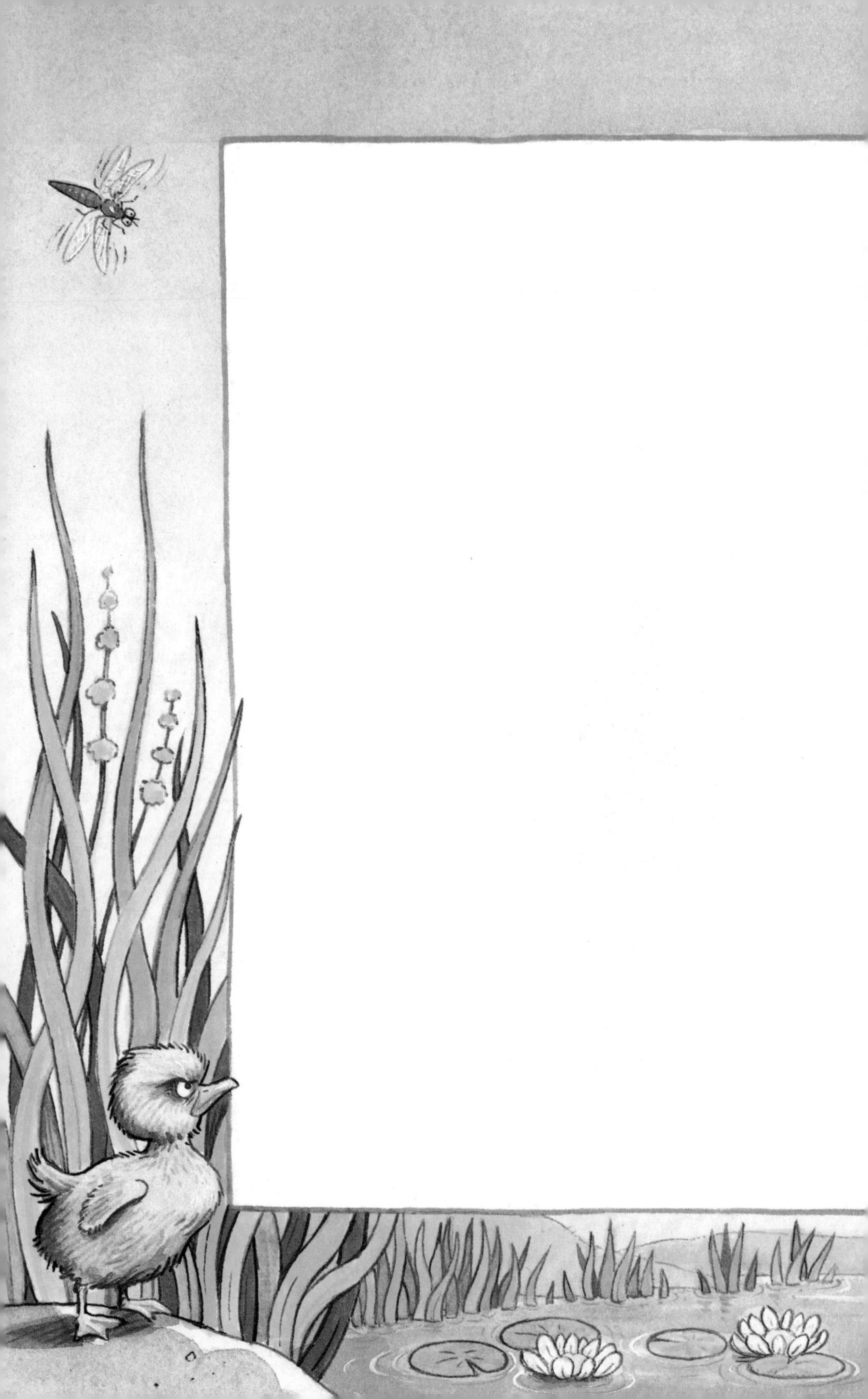

The Ugly Duckling

It was summer in the country. All the hay had been stacked, and the fields of wheat were yellow. Tall dock leaves grew on the banks of the canals.

Among the dock leaves, on her nest, sat a duck waiting for her eggs to hatch. She had been waiting for a long time.

At last the eggs began to crack and,
one by one, the ducklings
poked their heads out.

Before long, all the eggs had hatched except the biggest one. The duck sat a little longer, until out tumbled the last of her chicks.

But when she looked at him, she said, “Oh, dear! You’re so big and ugly.”

The next day was warm and sunny, so the duck took her new family down to the canal. She splashed into the water and, one by one, her ducklings followed her. Soon all of them were swimming beautifully, even the ugly grey one.

Next the ducklings went into the duck yard. “Stay close to me,” warned their mother. The other ducks thought the ducklings were beautiful – all except the big ugly one.

The ducklings stayed in the duck yard. But the ugly duckling was very unhappy there. The older ducks pecked at him and laughed. He had nowhere to hide, so one day he ran away.

He ran and ran until he came to the great marsh where the wild ducks lived. There he lay in the rushes for two whole weeks.

Then some wild ducks and some geese came to look at him. "You're *very* ugly," they said, and they laughed at him.

The poor little ugly duckling ran away from the great marsh. He ran and ran over fields and meadows. The wind blew and the rain rained. The duckling was cold, wet and very tired.

Just as it was getting dark, the duckling found a little cottage.

The cottage was very old and the door was falling off. This left a gap just big enough for the duckling to creep inside, out of the cold.

An old woman lived there. She had a cat that purred and a hen that laid eggs. She found the cold, starving little duckling in the morning.

The old woman looked at the duckling and said, "You can stay. Now we shall have duck eggs to eat, too!"

So the duckling stayed. But he *didn't* lay eggs.

The cat said to him, "Can you purr?"

"No," said the duckling.

The hen asked, "Can you lay eggs?"

"No," said the duckling, sadly.

"Then you must go," said the cat and the hen.

So the ugly duckling was alone once again. He walked in the marshes and floated on the water, and everywhere he went, all the birds and animals said, "How big and *ugly* you are."

Winter was coming. The leaves began to fall from the trees, and the ground was cold and hard.

The duckling had nowhere to stay.

One evening a flock of birds flew overhead. They were beautiful white swans with long necks.

"I wish *I* was like that," the duckling said sadly to himself.

He travelled on and on and the winter grew colder.

The ground froze and the duckling couldn't find food. One night, as he was pecking to find water, he was so tired that he fell asleep on the ice.

The next morning a farmer found the duckling and took him home so that his wife could take care of him.

As the duckling grew stronger, the farmer's children wanted to play with him. But the children were rough, and the duckling was frightened when they chased him. As soon as he could, he ran away again.

At last the duckling found a safe hiding place among the reeds in the marsh. There he stayed for the rest of the winter.

Then, after many long weeks, the warm spring sun began to shine again. The duckling spread his wings – they were strong wings now. Suddenly he rose from the ground and flew high into the air.

Down below, three beautiful swans were swimming on the canal. The duckling flew down to look at them. As he landed, the lonely bird saw his own reflection in the water.

He wasn't an ugly duckling at all! During the long winter he had grown into a beautiful white swan.

The other swans looked at him and admired his grace and beauty. "Come with us," they said.

And he did!

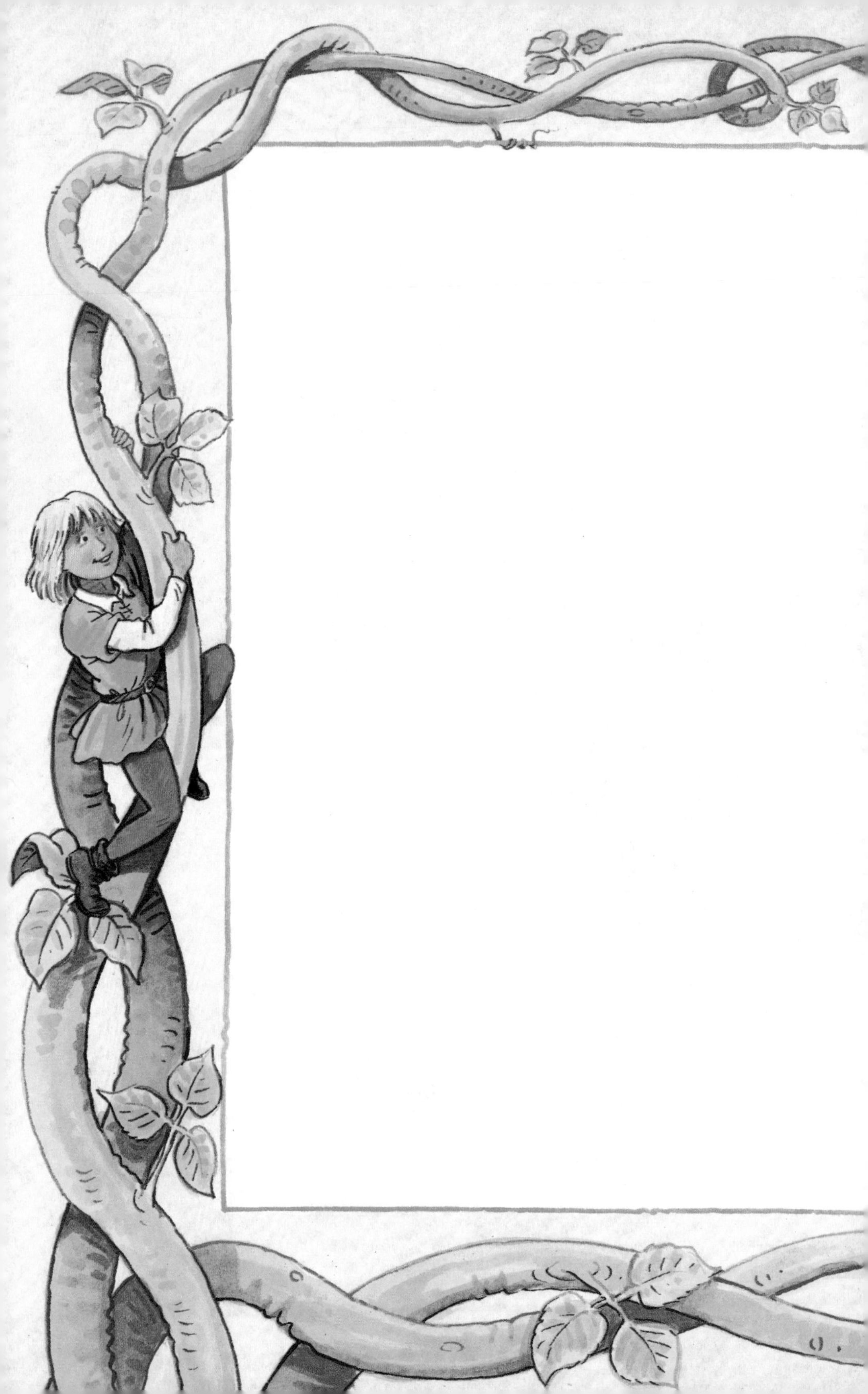

Jack and the Beanstalk

Once upon a time a boy named Jack lived with his mother. All they had in the world was one cow.

One day Jack's mother said, "We have no money for food. We shall have to sell the cow."

So Jack took the cow to market.
On the way, he met a man.

"If you give me your cow," said the man, "I'll give you some magic beans that are better than money."

Jack thought the magic beans sounded wonderful, so he gave the man the cow. Then he ran home as fast as he could.

"How much money did you get for the cow?" asked his mother.

"I got something much better than money," said Jack, showing her the magic beans.

"These beans are no good to us!" cried his mother angrily. And she threw them out of the window.

When Jack woke up the next day, his room seemed darker than usual. He went to the window and saw that a huge beanstalk had grown up in the garden overnight.

"I must find out what's at the top," he cried, rushing outside. And he began to climb the beanstalk.

Up and up he climbed. At last he found himself in a bare, rocky wilderness.

There were no plants or animals to be seen anywhere. But a long road led into the distance, and Jack began to walk along it. Towards evening he came to a castle and knocked loudly on the door.

"Could you give me some food and a bed for the night, please?" Jack asked the woman who answered.

"Oh no," said the woman. "My husband is a fierce giant who hates strangers." But Jack begged so hard that she let him in and gave him some supper.

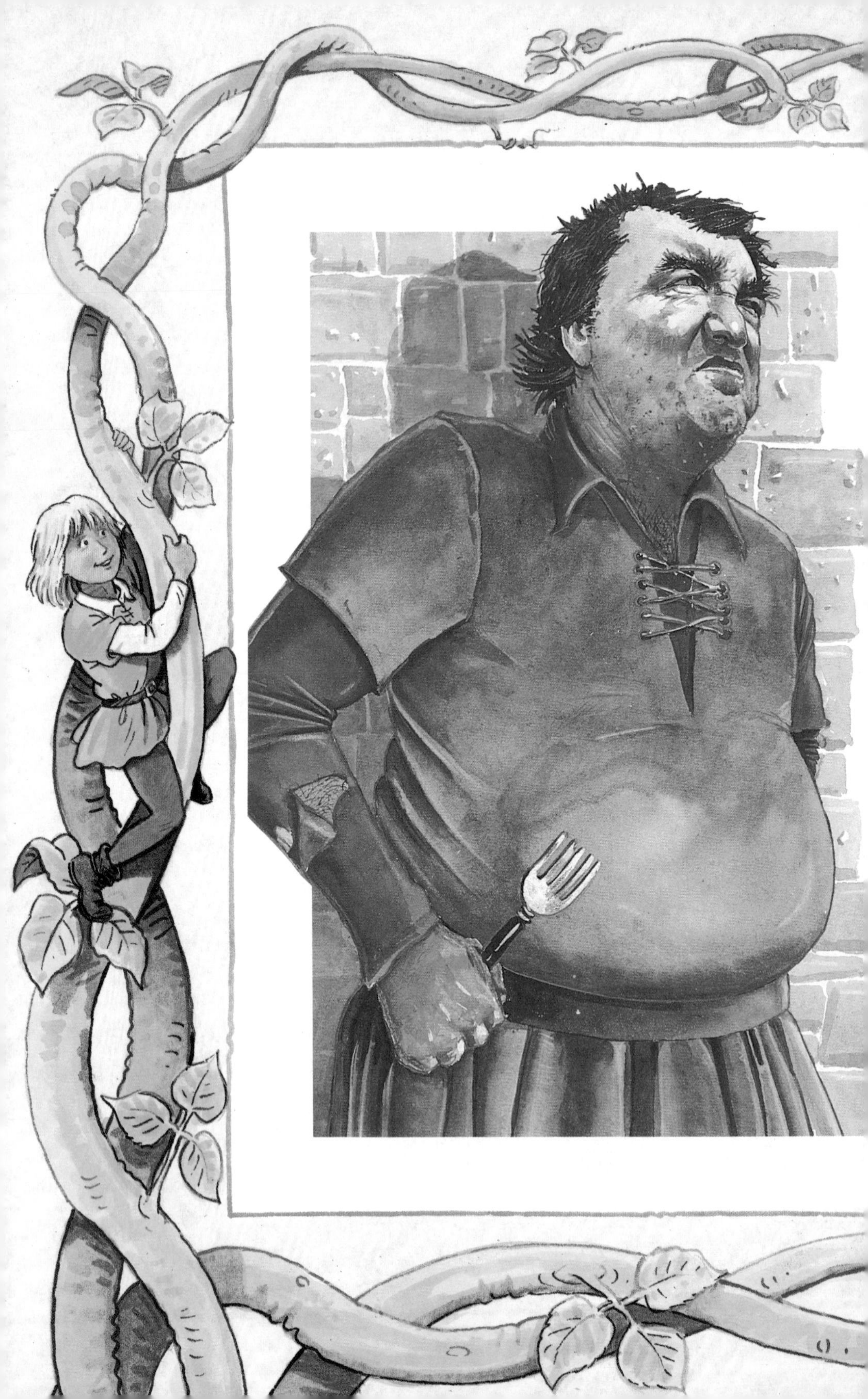

Just as Jack was enjoying some hot soup, he heard the giant coming. The woman quickly hid Jack in a cupboard.

The giant stalked in and roared,

"Fee, fie, foe, fum,
I smell the blood of an Englishman!
Be he alive or be he dead,
I'll grind his bones to make my bread!"

"Nonsense!" said his wife. "There's no one here." And she gave the giant his supper.

When he had finished his supper, the giant bellowed, “Bring me my hen!”

His wife brought a little hen and put it on the table.

“Lay!” shouted the giant.

Jack peeped out of his hiding place. To his amazement, every time the giant shouted, the hen laid a little golden egg.

When he had twelve golden eggs, the giant fell asleep.

As soon as all was quiet, Jack crept out of the cupboard, grabbed the little hen and tiptoed out.

Then he ran and ran until he was back at the top of the beanstalk. Quickly, he climbed down and took the magic hen to his mother.

How pleased she was! "Long ago, a wicked giant stole this hen from your father," she said. "Now that we have her back, our worries are over."

Jack lived happily with his mother for a while. But he longed for adventure, and one day he decided to climb the beanstalk again.

Just as before, Jack reached the castle towards evening. And once again the giant's wife hid him when they heard the giant roar,

"Fee, fie, foe, fum,
I smell the blood of an Englishman!
Be he alive or be he dead,
I'll grind his bones to make my bread!"

After supper the giant shouted, “Fetch me my money bags!” His wife brought him some sacks filled with gold coins.

The giant emptied the sacks onto the table and counted the coins over and over again. At last he put the money back in the sacks and fell asleep.

Quick as a flash, Jack took the money and ran all the way home.

His mother was delighted when she saw the money bags. "The giant stole this money from your father," she said. "You have done well to bring it back."

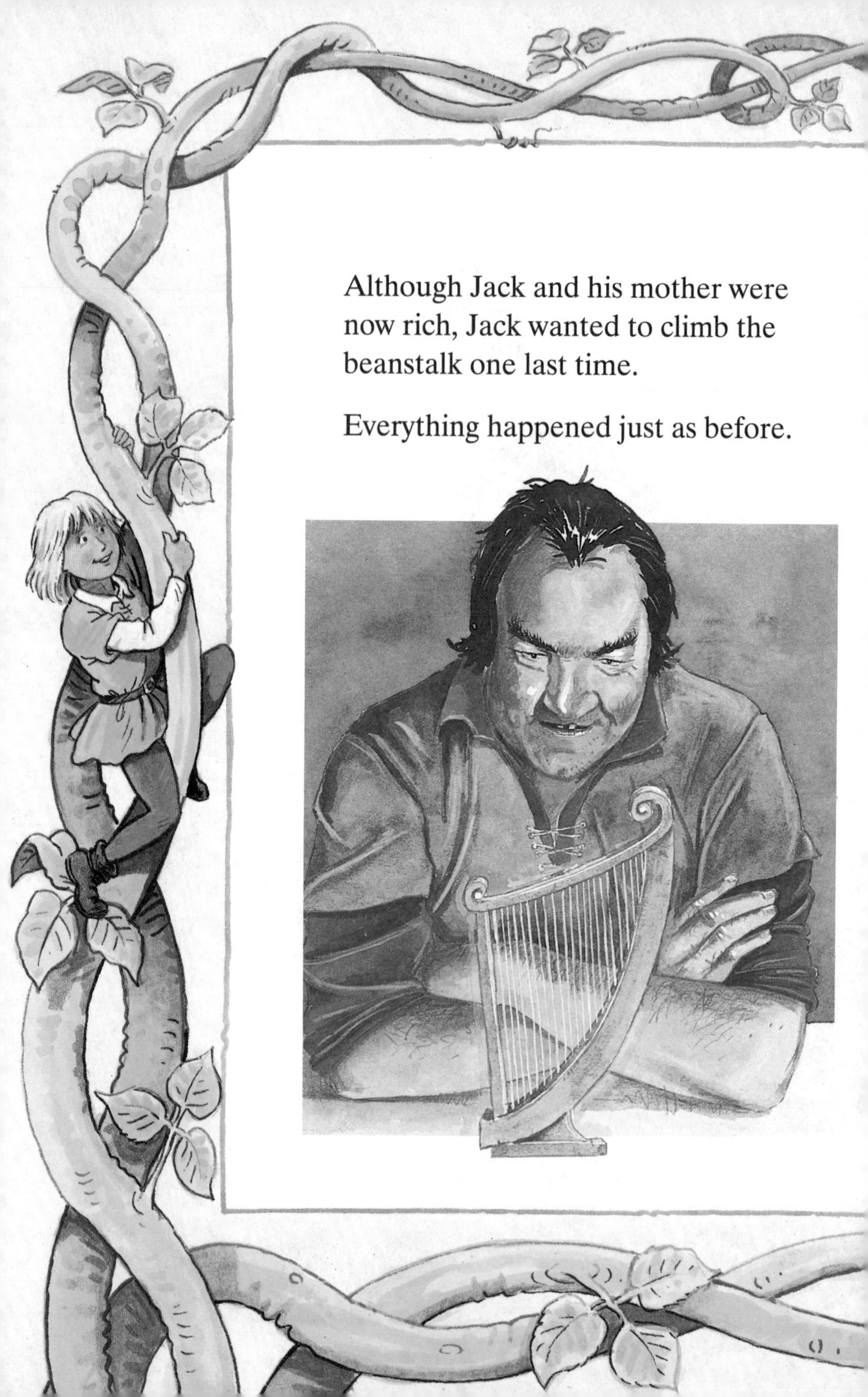

Although Jack and his mother were now rich, Jack wanted to climb the beanstalk one last time.

Everything happened just as before.

This time the giant's wife brought a beautiful golden harp. "Play!" roared the giant, and the harp began to play soft music.

The music was so gentle that it sent the giant to sleep. But when Jack crept out and seized it, the harp cried, "Master! Master!"

The giant woke up in a rage, just in time to see Jack disappearing through the door with the harp. “Stop, thief!” the giant roared.

Now Jack had to run for his life. The giant took huge strides and was soon hard on Jack’s heels. Scrambling down the beanstalk, Jack shouted as loudly as he could, “Mother, Mother, bring the axe!”

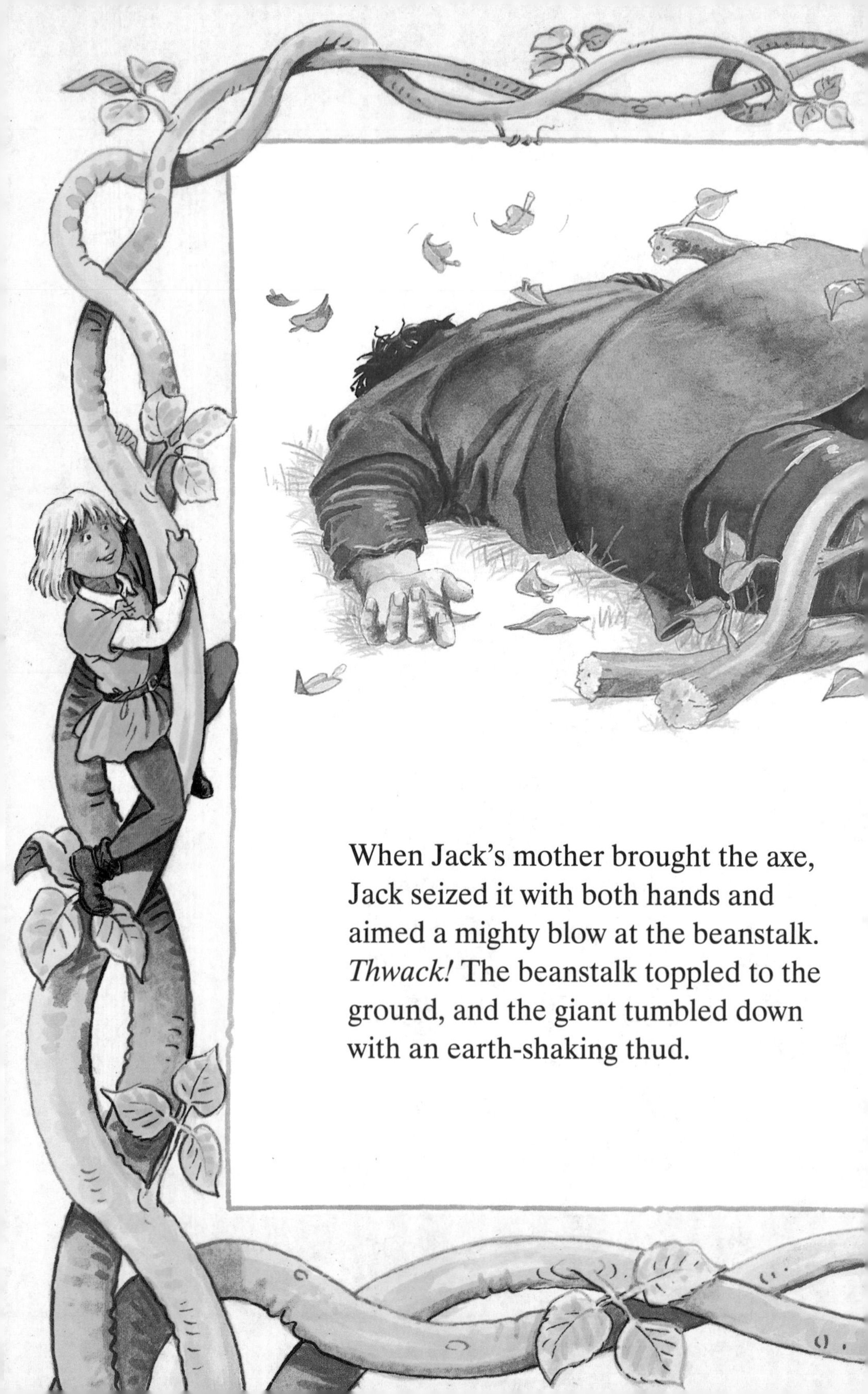

When Jack's mother brought the axe, Jack seized it with both hands and aimed a mighty blow at the beanstalk. *Thwack!* The beanstalk toppled to the ground, and the giant tumbled down with an earth-shaking thud.

So that was the end of the giant.
Jack and his mother were never poor
again, and they both lived happily
ever after.

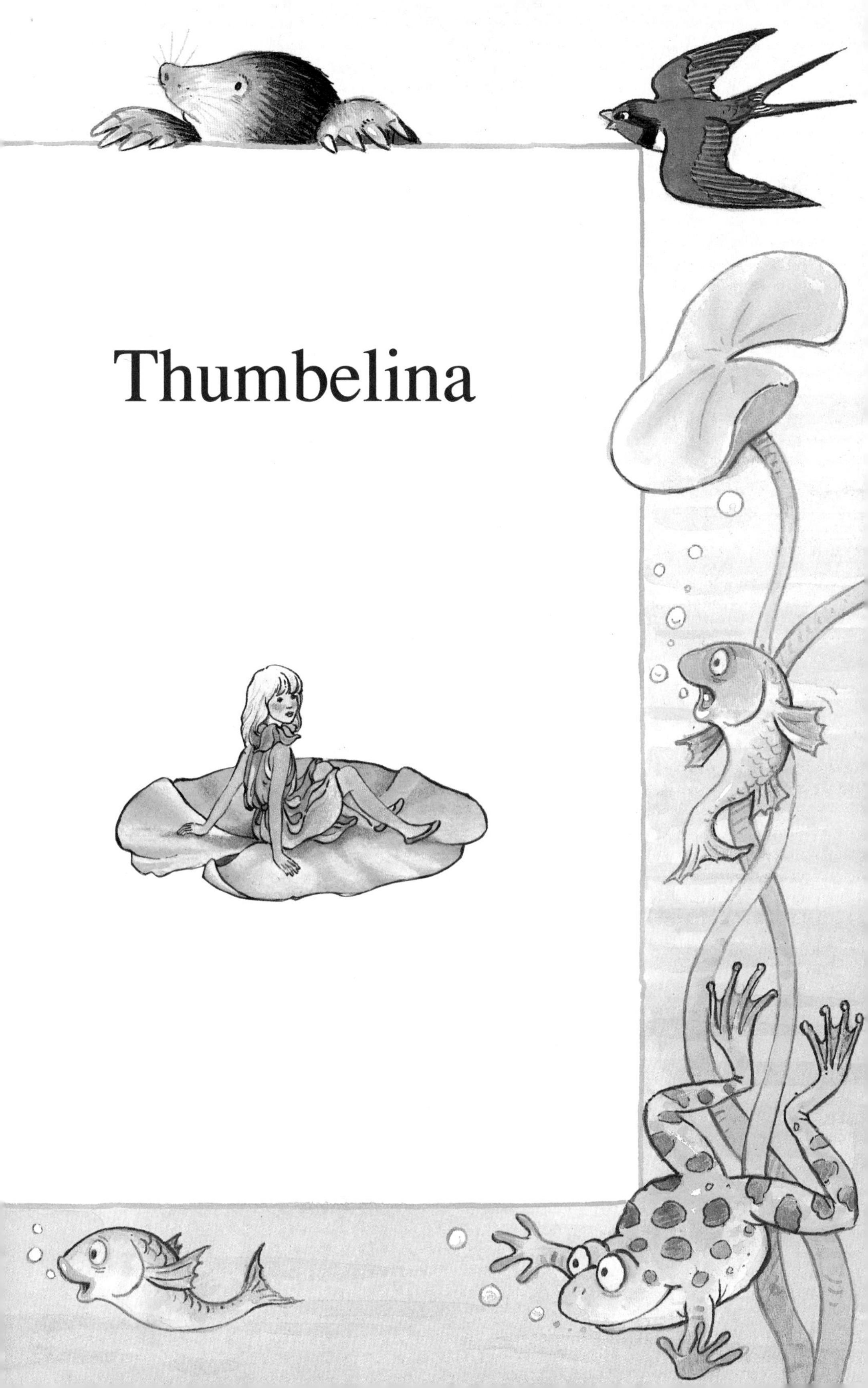

Thumbelina

Once upon a time there was a woman who longed to have a little girl of her own to love and care for. As time passed, and she had no children, she became very sad.

Then one day she heard of a wise old woman who could help, and she went to see her.

The wise old woman smiled. "Take this tiny seed and plant it in a flower pot," she said, "and you will have your little girl."

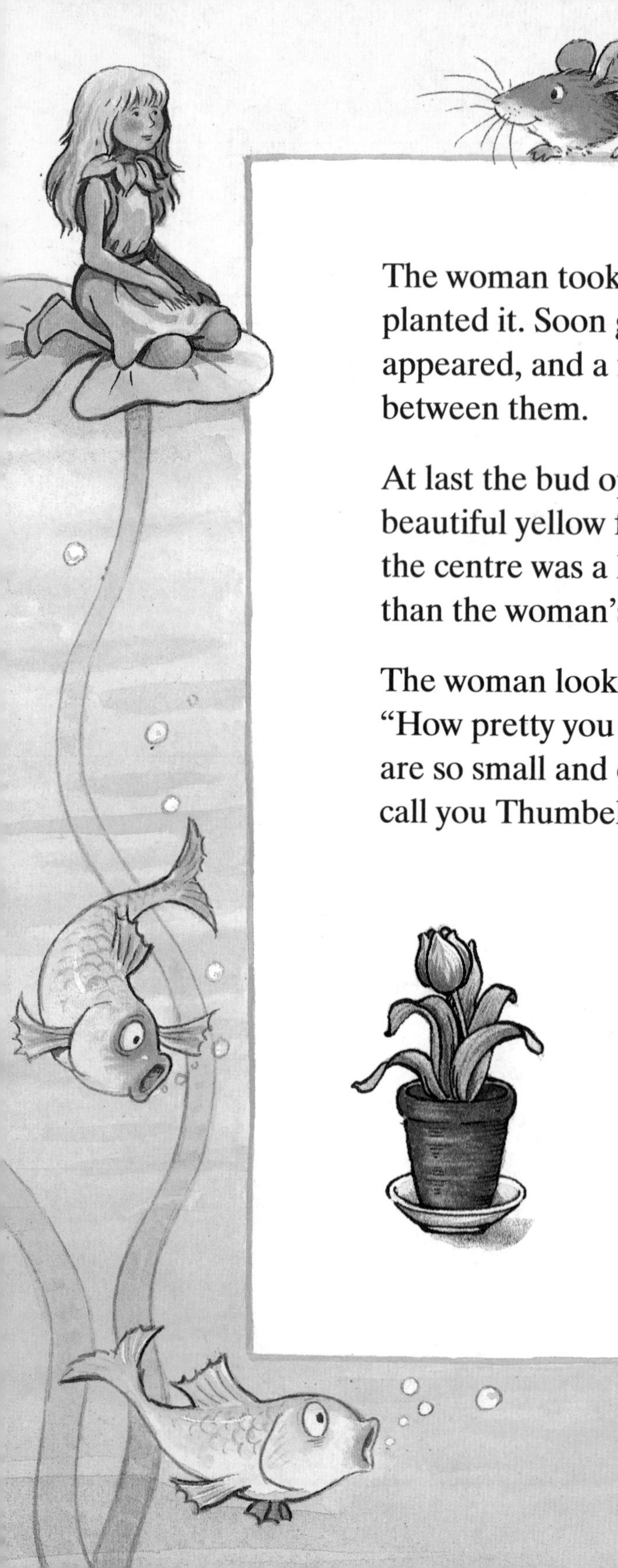

The woman took the seed home and planted it. Soon green shoots appeared, and a flower bud grew between them.

At last the bud opened out into a beautiful yellow flower. And right in the centre was a little girl, no bigger than the woman's thumb.

The woman looked down at the girl. "How pretty you are!" she said. "You are so small and dainty, I'm going to call you Thumbelina."

The woman was happy to have a little girl at last, and she took good care of Thumbelina.

Thumbelina was happy too. She sang songs in her soft, clear voice as she played on the kitchen table. At night she slept in a bed made from a tiny walnut shell.

Then one day a big toad heard Thumbelina's singing and hopped in through the window. "What a pretty wife you would make for my son!" she said. And she carried Thumbelina away to the stream where she lived.

The toad left the tiny girl all alone on a lily leaf and went off to find her son.

Thumbelina didn't want to marry an ugly toad at all, but she didn't know how she could escape.

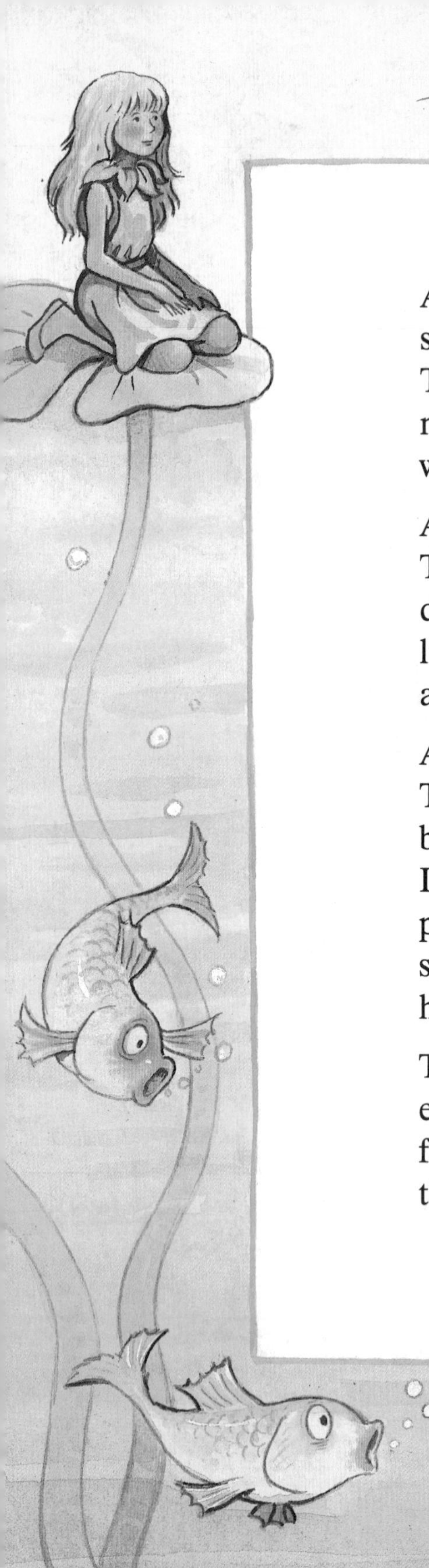

After a while some friendly fish came swimming by. “Please help me,” Thumbelina begged. “The toad wants me to marry her son. I must find a way to escape!”

All the fish felt very sorry for Thumbelina. So they spent the whole day nibbling through the stem of the lily leaf, and at last Thumbelina was able to float away.

As she drifted down the stream, Thumbelina met a beautiful butterfly. It took her to a pleasant wood where she could make a home for herself.

Thumbelina was happy in the wood, eating the nuts and berries that she found, and playing with her friends the butterflies.

But soon the days grew colder. When winter came, it was harder for Thumbelina to find food. Her friends the butterflies disappeared, and she was alone.

Then one day Thumbelina met a friendly fieldmouse who was just going into her little house.

“I’m so hungry,” Thumbelina said. “Please can you help me?”

The fieldmouse took pity on the girl. “Of course,” she said. “You can stay with me in my warm house and share my food.”

Thumbelina lived happily with the fieldmouse for a long time. But one day the fieldmouse said, “I can’t keep you here much longer. Why don’t you marry my friend the mole, who lives next door? He has a much bigger house than mine. And he will look after you next winter.”

Thumbelina did not want to marry the mole. He lived under the ground and knew nothing of the sunny world outside.

Next day the mole visited Thumbelina.
"Please come and see where I live,"
he said.

Thumbelina did not want to hurt the mole's feelings, so she followed him into the tunnel that led to his dark underground home.

"Be careful," said the mole. "There is a dead bird just here."

Thumbelina saw that the bird was a swallow. He was not dead, just very cold and weak.

Thumbelina felt sorry for the swallow.
She covered him with dried leaves
and grass to keep him warm.

Thumbelina looked after the swallow all through the long, cold winter. By summer he was strong and well and ready to go back to his own home.

Thumbelina said goodbye to the swallow as he flew off with his friends. She was happy that he was well, but she knew that she would miss him. And she was sad to think that before the next winter came, she would have to marry the mole and live underground.

When summer ended, Thumbelina looked up at the sky for the last time with tears in her eyes. Birds were flying high overhead, and suddenly one of them swooped down to her. It was the swallow she had saved!

"I am going to a warm country," he told her. "Come with me."

Thumbelina was overjoyed. She climbed onto the swallow's back and flew with him to a faraway land where it was always summer.

This land was full of flowers. And inside every one lived a tiny person, just like Thumbelina!

"We are the Flower People," they said, "and this is your true home. We will call you Maia."

Maia loved her new home. Before long, she married the handsome Prince of the Flower People, and they lived happily ever after.